Deep Thinker And The Stars

Story by
Patricia Murdoch
Illustrations by
Kellie Jobson

Three Trees Press

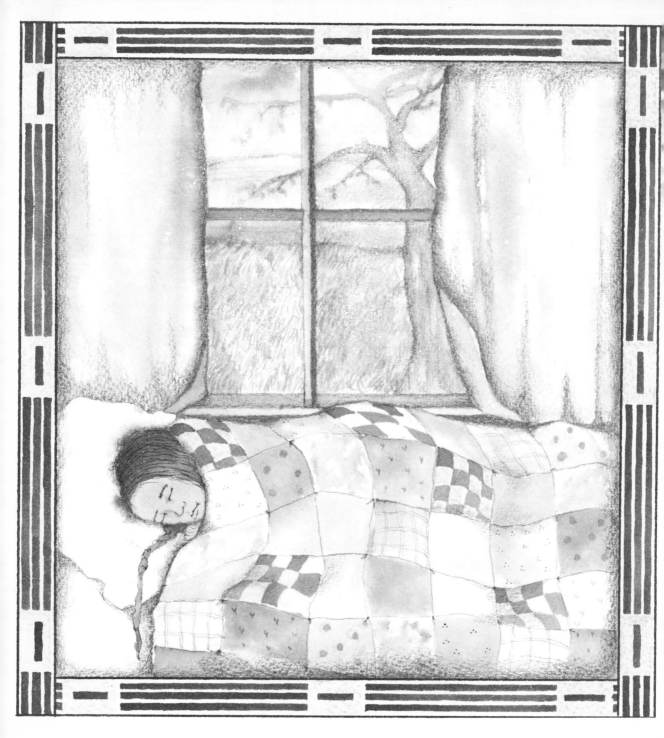

A cold wind blew across the frozen lake and whistled at the cabin window. Sharon lay snuggled under her quilts, listening to it howl.

"Time to get up, Deep Thinker," her grandmother called.
Sharon held her breath and threw the covers off. She shivered as
her toes touched the bare floor. Quickly she pulled her moccasins out
from under her bed and put them on.

She heard her mother and father talking excitedly in the kitchen. She opened the curtain and felt the warmth from the wood stove on her face.

"Is today the day?" she asked.

"Now how did you know that?" her father teased.

Her mother smiled and patted her large tummy. "I'll be flying to the hospital on this morning's plane."

Sharon tried to wrap her arms around her, but her mother was too big.

"The baby's finally going to come out," she said, resting her head on her mother's tummy.

Sharon's grandmother brushed and braided Sharon's long black hair while she ate her breakfast. The warm bread and sweet tea tasted good.

"I have something to show you," her grandmother said. "Do you remember this?" She showed Sharon a wooden cradleboard covered with blue and white blankets. "Your mother carried you in this until you were a year old."

Sharon giggled. "I was too small to remember, Grandma."

"Of course you were. The new baby will use this now." She touched the curved edges. "Your grandfather carved it. I remember him working long into the night. We didn't have electricity then, so he had to see by the light of the fire. The light would dance and sway...." She brushed tears from her eyes.

"Oh Grandma, I wish Grandad were still alive." Sharon sighed. "If only I could think of a way for the baby to know him."

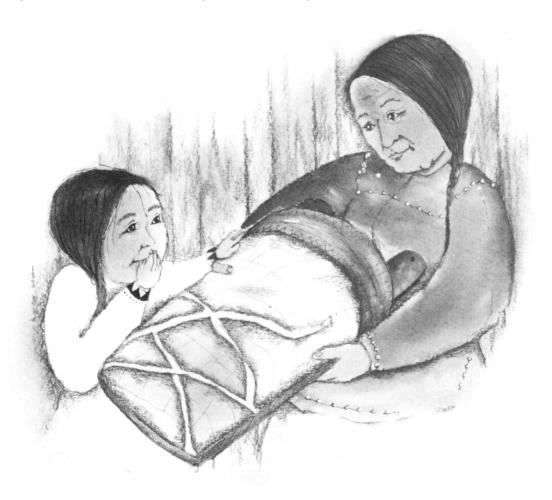

"Time to go." her father said. "The plane won't wait for anyone in this cold." He took the cradleboard and suitcase outside and put them in the ski-doo sled.

Sharon's mother stroked her cheek. "When it was time for you to be born, your father was in the bush trapping. Your grandfather took me across the lake to the airport in his boat. I'll never forget how the water sparkled in the sun, like a thousand diamonds. I was so happy — and so scared." She kissed Sharon on the forehead. "It's been very lonely without him these last few weeks."

Sharon felt funny when her mother was sad. She wished she could make her feel better, but she couldn't think how. She tried not to cry as she waved goodbye.

The next morning, Sharon's grandmother showed her how to string brightly coloured beads for necklaces. At suppertime, her mother phoned. Sharon had a new baby brother!

They were so happy that her father played his guitar and they sang until bedtime.

When Sharon was tucked under her quilts, she called to her father. "What's the baby's name going to be?"

He sat on the edge of her bed and gently tugged on her braids.

"Well, he will have two names," he answered. "One that we will call him all the time and his special name."

"Grandma called me my special name this morning. She said, 'Get up, Deep Thinker.' Tell me how I got my special name again. Please Daddy?"

"Grandad gave you your name when you were only a few weeks old. He held you in his arms and you looked him right in the eye, far longer than most babies could. 'This girl is thinking already,' he said. 'I feel as though she knows me through and through. Her name will be Deep Thinker.'"

He kissed her on the forehead. "Grandad had been looking forward to naming this baby too...." Her father stopped talking and looked out the window. Sharon saw his lip tremble.

"Oh Daddy," she whispered, and hugged him.

After her father said goodnight, Sharon pulled the covers high up under her chin and thought of her grandfather. She remembered the wrinkled brown face with the wonderful eyes, the eyes that had diamonds in them.

It would be a week before the hospital would let Sharon's mother bring the baby home. Her grandmother taught Sharon how to take the long strands of beads and make them into different shapes. Sharon worked quietly all week.

"Watch carefully and I'll show you how to make a star," her grandmother said.

Sharon watched and then tried, but her threads got tangled. She pulled and pulled until the threads snapped and the beads flew across the room.

"Stupid, stupid beads," she said, jabbing the needle into the pin cushion.

"Ah, Deep Thinker, what is troubling you? Do you miss your mother?"

"She's been gone so long, Grandma." Sharon wiped her nose and began to gather up the beads.

"I know it's hard when someone's gone, but she'll be home soon, with your new brother."

Finally, the day came for mother to come home. The moment she entered the house, Sharon rushed to her with her arms open wide.

Her mother carefully took the cradleboard off her back. She opened the blankets that were protecting the baby's face. Sharon lightly touched his fat cheeks and soft black hair.

The baby yawned.

"Oh Mom, he's beautiful."

"You were a beautiful baby too."

When the baby was tucked into his hammock, Sharon swung him gently. She kissed him on the cheek. He opened his eyes, blinked, and gave a little smile. Sharon felt a tingling in her stomach. She had seen those eyes before! The baby had the eyes of her grandfather!

A few days later, Sharon's mother and grandmother started getting ready for the feast where her brother would receive his special name. They cooked moosemeat stew and bannock and cakes.

The night before the feast, Sharon woke when everyone was still asleep. Very quietly, she got out of bed and took her beads to the couch. She sat in the moonlight and worked and worked until she had made two tiny stars. The sun started to come up as she tiptoed back to bed.

As relatives and friends began arriving for the naming ceremony, Sharon wrapped the stars up in a piece of cloth and hid them in the baby's blankets.

When everyone arrived, her grandmother sat with the baby by the stove.

"There is something special about this child," she said. "His eyes are comforting. They make one's heart calm and still." She lifted him up and the package fell out of his blankets.

Grandmother opened the cloth and took out the two silvery stars.

She held them up to the light, where they sparkled and danced.

"This reminds me of the time ..." She said slowly.

"Ah, Deep Thinker, you are wise beyond your years. The stars you have made are the stars in this child's eyes and the brightness we remember your grandfather with. This boy's name will be the 'Boy with the Stars in His Eyes.'"

Sharon wanted to laugh and cry and hide, all at the same time. Her father put his arm around her.

"Thank you child" he whispered. "Now we can remember your grandfather, but without the sadness."

Her mother bent down, so that her face was very close to Sharon's. "I'll sew the stars to his cradleboard tomorrow and we will have them forever," she said and kissed her.

Before Sharon went to bed, she opened her curtains. She looked out at the glistening snow and thought of her grandfather, her baby brother, and the stars she had made.

Deep Thinker smiled.

Canadian Cataloguing in Publication Data

Murdoch, Patricia
    Deep Thinker and the Stars

ISBN 0-88823-127-X (bound)   –   ISBN 0-88823-125-3 (pbk.)

I. Jobson, Kellie.   II. Title.

PS8576.U75D43 1987   jC813'.54   C87-094231-X
PZ7.M86De 1987

ISBN 0-88823-125-3 pb
ISBN 0-88823-127-X hc

Story© 1987 Patricia Murdoch
Illustrations© 1987 Kellie Jobson

All rights reserved
Published by Three Trees Press
85 King Street East
Toronto, Ontario M5C 1G3

Printed and bound in Canada

Published with the assistance of the Canada Council and the Ontario Arts Council